WHEN UNICORNS POOP

by Lexie Castle

Illustrated by Christian Cornia

RP|KIDS
PHILADELPHIA

To my Glittering "Rainbow" Tommy and
to my Lovely "Unicorn Mom" Erika
—C.C.

Running Press Kids
Hachette Book Group
1290 Avenue of the Americas, New York, NY 10104
www.runningpress.com/rpkids
@RP_Kids

Printed in China

First Edition: October 2019

Published by Running Press Kids, an imprint of Perseus Books, LLC, a subsidiary of Hachette Book Group, Inc. The Running Press Kids name and logo is a trademark of the Hachette Book Group.

Print book cover and interior design by Frances J. Soo Ping Chow.

Library of Congress Control Number: 2018959366

ISBNs: 978-0-7624-6712-9 (hardcover), 978-0-7624-6711-2 (ebook), 978-0-7624-6738-9 (ebook), 978-0-7624-6739-6 (ebook)

APS

10 9 8 7 6 5 4 3 2 1

When unicorns poop . . .

colorful rainbows arch through the sky.

When unicorns sneeze . . .

sparkly glitter bedazzles coats and shoes.

When unicorns spit . . .

chocolate syrup drizzles over sweet sundaes.

When unicorns toot . . .

shiny bubbles float through flowery gardens.

When unicorns puke . . .

bright ribbons dance in the cheerful breeze.

When unicorns cry . . .

sugary milkshakes fill fancy glasses.

When unicorns shout . . .

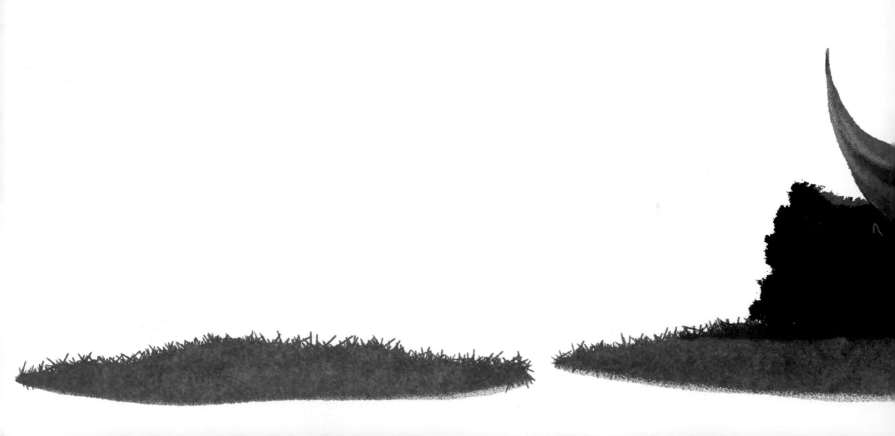

dazzling fireworks explode, lighting up the sky.

When you find a band of unicorns,
you can throw a party!

But remember . . .

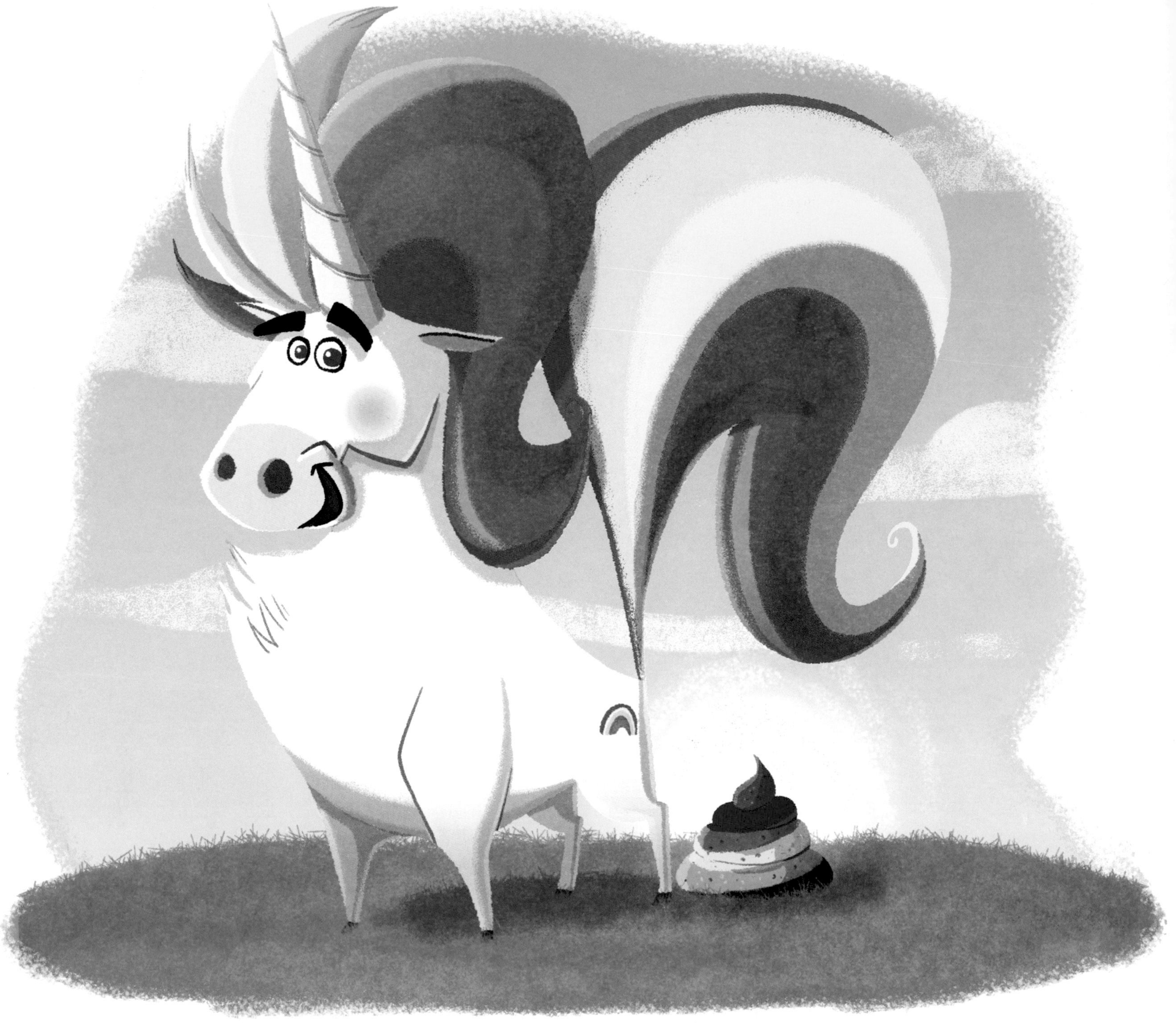

don’t step in their poop.